PEACHTREE

GRIDIRON BULLY

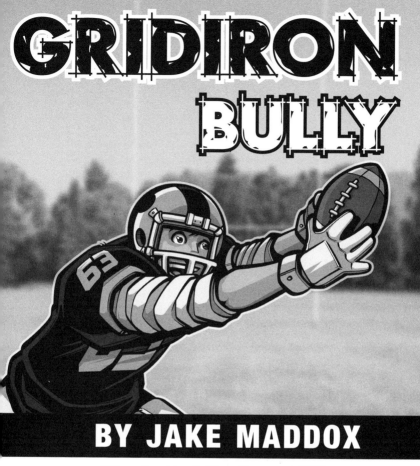

BY JAKE MADDOX

illustrated by Sean Tiffany

text by Chris Kreie

Impact Books are published by Stone Arch Books
151 Good Counsel Drive, P.O. Box 669
Mankato, Minnesota 56002
www.stonearchbooks.com

Library of Congress Cataloging-in-Publication Data
Maddox, Jake.

    Gridiron Bully / by Jake Maddox; illustrated by Sean Tiffany.
    p. cm. — (Impact Books. A Jake Maddox Sports Story)
    ISBN 978-1-4342-1201-6 (library binding)
    ISBN 978-1-4342-1399-0 (pbk.)
    [1. Football—Fiction.] I. Tiffany, Sean, ill. II. Title.
PZ7.M25643Gr 2009
[Fic]—dc22   2008031955

Summary:
Juan was a track star at his old school, so he's not sure what to expect
when he's asked to join the football team in his new town. Right away,
Juan thinks he's made the wrong choice. He can't catch, he can't throw,
and one of the members of the team hasn't been making it easy for Juan
to feel at home. Can the ex-track star learn his new sport in time for the
biggest game of the season?

Creative Director: Heather Kindseth
Graphic Designer: Carla Zetina-Yglesias

1 2 3 4 5 6 14 13 12 11 10 09

Printed in the United States of America

TABLE OF CONTENTS

CHAPTER 1

DISCOVERED

Under the hot August sun, Juan ran as fast as a racecar across the black surface of the school track. He was running alone, with no one to push him but himself. He was trying to improve his best time on the 200-meter sprint.

Juan's legs pumped. *Relax, breathe, take long strides*, he thought. *Relax, breathe, take long strides*. Finally, he pushed his body across the finish line.

After jogging a few more steps, Juan lay down flat on his back on the hard track. His heart raced. Sweat trickled down his face onto the rough pavement. He stared up at the sky and tried to catch his breath.

All he could hear, besides his heartbeat, were the noises of the football team practicing on the field in the center of the track. Suddenly, the face of his little sister, Lydia, blocked Juan's view of the sky. She was holding a stopwatch.

"24.81 seconds," said Lydia. "Not bad."

"Not that good, either," said Juan. He pushed himself up and looked at the football field. A man was there, waving at them.

"Hey kid!" shouted the man. "Come over here."

Juan and Lydia looked at each other, then back at the man. "Is he talking to us?" Juan asked his sister.

"Yeah, you!" yelled the man.

Juan and Lydia jogged over to him. The man stuck out his hand. "I'm Coach Bryant," he said.

Juan shook his hand. "I'm Juan."

"Nice to meet you, Juan," said Coach Bryant.

"And this is my sister, Lydia," said Juan.

"I'm ten," said Lydia. "I'm going into fifth grade."

Coach Bryant smiled. "And how about you, Juan?" he asked. "What grade will you be in this fall?"

"Seventh," said Juan.

"Perfect," said Coach Bryant. "That's the seventh-grade football team behind me, the Raiders. You should think about playing. I was watching you sprint. You're fast."

"Juan set a state record in Montana for the 200-meter race," Lydia said.

"Be quiet, Lydia," Juan told her.

"Is that right?" asked Coach Bryant. "Montana, huh?"

"Yeah," said Lydia. "We just moved here from Montana last week."

"You don't have to tell him our whole life story," Juan said.

"That's okay," Coach Bryant said, laughing. "Did you play football back in Montana, Juan?"

"My school didn't have a team," said Juan. "I was just on the track team."

"Well, that doesn't matter," said Coach Bryant. "I can teach you. I coach the wide receivers and defensive backs. We could use a super-fast guy like you on the team."

"I'll think about it," said Juan.

"Good," said Coach Bryant. "If you show up tomorrow morning at 8 o'clock, I'll have a uniform and a set of pads waiting for you."

"I have to watch my sister," Juan told him.

"Bring Lydia along," Coach Bryant said. "We'll find something for her to do."

"He'll be there," said Lydia.

Coach Bryant laughed. "Great," he said. "I'll see you both tomorrow."

CHAPTER 2

FIRST PRACTICE

The next morning, Juan and Lydia walked through the gate of the football field. Dozens of kids were already there, warming up.

"Hey, Juan! Over here!" Coach Bryant yelled.

Juan and Lydia headed over to him. "Hi," Juan said.

"I'm glad you came," said Coach Bryant.

Two boys were standing next to him. "Juan, meet Anthony and Reggie," the coach said. "Anthony is a wide receiver and defensive back."

"The best wide receiver and defensive back," said Anthony.

Coach Bryant ignored him and pointed at the other guy. "And Reggie's our quarterback," the coach went on.

"How's it going?" said Reggie.

"Ready to get started right away?" asked Coach Bryant.

"I'm ready," Juan said.

"What about me?" Lydia asked.

"How would you like to be my assistant?" Coach Bryant asked her.

"Okay!" Lydia said.

"Great," Coach Bryant said. "Your first job as my assistant is to go get some water bottles for us." He pointed across the field. Lydia started running.

"Let's get started," said Coach Bryant. "Juan, for this first drill, run about five steps, then stop and turn toward the middle of the field to catch the ball. I'll throw to you. Reggie, you throw to Anthony."

Juan and Anthony got ready. Reggie and Coach Bryant each held a football.

"Hut!" yelled Coach Bryant.

Anthony exploded down the sideline. He came to a quick stop, turned, and then caught the ball that Reggie threw to him. Juan just watched.

"Juan," said Coach Bryant, "you were supposed to go."

"Oh," said Juan. "Sorry."

Anthony ran up with the football. "Rookie doesn't even know what hut means," he said, laughing. Reggie laughed, too, and gave Anthony a high five.

"Let's try it again," said Coach Bryant.

Juan and Anthony lined up. "Hut!" the coach yelled.

That time, Juan sprinted forward. He tried to remember what the coach had told him to do. He stopped and quickly turned to his right, away from the middle of the field. The ball sailed past him.

"Turn toward the middle of the field!" yelled Coach Bryant. "The middle!"

"Sorry, Coach," said Juan. He ran to get the ball.

"Let's try something else," Coach Bryant said when Juan returned. "This time, run straight down the field. Look back after thirty yards, and I'll hit you with the ball."

"Got it," said Juan. He pushed down on his helmet to make sure it was tight. Then he thought of something. "Um, how far is thirty yards?" he asked.

Anthony and Reggie laughed.

"You cross six of the lines on the field," said the coach. "The lines are five yards apart."

"Got it," said Juan.

"Okay," said Coach Bryant. "Hut!"

Juan took off. As he ran, he counted to himself, "One line, two lines, three, four, five, six." Then he turned around.

The ball was already in the air. Juan slowed down, but the ball didn't. It flew over his head and landed past him.

"Okay!" shouted the coach. "Bring it in."

Juan picked up the ball. Then he followed Anthony back.

"Maybe you should stay on the track," said Anthony. "Anyone can run. But football takes skills."

"Juan, you've got to keep running," said Coach Bryant. "You have to catch the ball."

"Sorry, Coach," said Juan, looking down at the ground.

"You'll figure it out," said Coach Bryant. "Don't worry about it. Go get some water."

Juan ran to the sidelines. Lydia was waiting there with a water bottle.

"You'll catch the next one," Lydia said, holding out the bottle.

Juan was sweating. He took off his helmet and poured water over his head to cool off. As the water ran down his face, he closed his eyes and tried to picture what it would be like to actually catch a football.

CHAPTER 3

HEAD TO HEAD

After dinner that night, Lydia and Juan went back to the football field to practice. Lydia stood, ready to toss Juan a ball. Juan ran across the field and tried to remember the different drills he'd learned at football practice that day.

Juan sprinted ten yards. Then he turned and ran across the football field. Lydia fired a tennis ball directly at him. Juan reached up and grabbed it out of the air.

Juan jogged back over to his sister. "I wish you could throw a football," he said.

"Well, I can't," said Lydia. "It's like throwing a giant egg."

Juan laughed. "Yeah, it's a funny shape," he said. He reached over and messed up Lydia's hair.

"Aw, isn't that cute?" someone yelled. Juan turned around. Anthony and Reggie were walking toward them.

"Look, Rookie's practicing with his baby sister," said Anthony.

Reggie just smiled. "Too bad we don't use tennis balls in real games," Anthony said. "And too bad we don't play against a bunch of little girls. We'll see how he does against real competition when we play the Giants on Saturday. Come on, Reggie."

Anthony and Reggie brushed past Juan. They headed toward the other end of the field.

"Hold on," Juan said. "Why don't we see how I do against some real competition right now?"

Anthony and Reggie stopped and turned around. "Do you mean what I think you mean?" Anthony asked.

"That's right," said Juan. "You and me. Head to head."

Anthony looked at Reggie and let out a big laugh. "Rookie thinks he can take me on," he said. "Okay, Rookie. Let's go."

Juan leaned over to Lydia. "Wish me luck," he whispered.

"Good luck," Lydia whispered back. "You can take him."

Juan walked toward Reggie and put his toes on the 20-yard line, facing Anthony. Anthony stared him down. Juan stretched his arms. Then he jogged in place for a few steps to try to calm down. Finally, he waited for the signal from Reggie.

"Hut!" yelled Reggie.

Juan sprinted forward. But all of a sudden, Anthony stepped in front of him and shoved him to the ground.

"Hey, that's not fair!" yelled Lydia.

Juan got to his feet. "Dude, what was that?" he asked.

"It's called a jam," said Reggie.

Anthony laughed. "Jams are okay to do within five yards of the line of scrimmage," he said.

"Let's do it again," said Reggie.

Juan lined up again. He looked across at Anthony and took a deep breath.

"Hut!" Reggie called.

Juan took off. He made a quick move around Anthony to avoid the jam. Then he kicked his legs into gear.

Juan flew down the field. Anthony tried to run with him, but he couldn't keep up. He kept getting farther and farther behind. Finally, the moment was just right, Juan looked over his shoulder. The ball was cruising through the air.

Keep running, he thought. His legs pushed his body forward as he watched the ball fall from the sky.

He was in the perfect position. At just the right instant, he reached out his arms.

But the ball came down too fast. It fell straight between Juan's outstretched hands and dropped to the ground.

Juan lost his balance. Suddenly, he felt like his legs were tangled. He crashed to the ground in a heap.

Anthony, Reggie, and Lydia all ran to him. They stood over Juan. He slowly sat up and shook his head.

"That was awesome," said Lydia.

"It's only awesome when you actually catch the ball," said Anthony. He added, "The track star should stay on the track. Let's get out of here, Reggie." Anthony turned and started walking away.

"You've got some wheels, Rookie," said Reggie. "You're fast. Just keep working on the hands. You'll get it. See you around."

Reggie ran after Anthony. Juan flopped on his back.

"You'll catch it next time," said Lydia.

"Yeah," said Juan. He took a deep breath. "Next time."

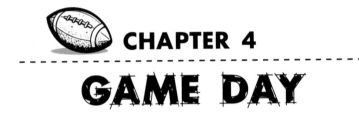

CHAPTER 4

GAME DAY

Saturday was game day. The Raiders were taking on the Central Giants.

Juan sat on the bench and watched as his teammates headed out to the field. Coach Bryant patted him on the shoulder pads. "You'll get in there soon," he said.

But Juan didn't mind. He was relieved to be sitting on the bench. His nerves were on fire. He didn't think he was ready to be on the field.

Juan watched as the Raiders moved down the field against the Giants. On the final play of the drive, Reggie faked a handoff to the running back. Then he ran to his right and fired a pass to Anthony in the end zone. It was a quick touchdown. After the extra point, the Raiders were ahead 7–0.

On the next drive, the Giants ran a few good plays. Then Anthony stepped in front of a pass and intercepted the ball. Now it was the Raiders' ball.

"Juan!" yelled Coach Bryant. "Go in!"

"What?" Juan said, surprised.

"You're in!" Coach Bryant said. "Get out there."

Juan jumped up and raced onto the field. He joined the Raiders in their huddle.

Reggie told the offense what play they were going to run. "Break," said the rest of the team. The Raiders ran to the line of scrimmage.

Juan's heart was pounding and his mind was racing. He tried to picture the play in his head.

Just run diagonally toward the middle of the field, he told himself. *That's all I have to do.*

Reggie shouted at the line, "Hut one! Hut two!"

The players burst forward. Juan ran two steps. Then a Giants player hammered him to the ground.

Anthony caught a pass from Reggie and got tackled near the 20-yard line.

The next play was a running play. The running back got the handoff from Reggie.

Then the running back ran to Juan's side of the field. Juan tried putting a block on the defender in front of him, but again, he was pushed to the ground — hard.

Juan climbed back up and ran to the huddle. His body hurt from the hard hits.

In the huddle, Reggie told the team the next play. It was another pass play.

"Break," said the Raiders.

At the line of scrimmage, Juan leaned forward. His heart was still pounding. He looked down the line at Reggie.

"Hut one!" Reggie shouted.

Juan exploded off the line. He ran fast into the end zone. Then he stopped and turned toward the middle of the field. Reggie spotted him and let the ball fly.

Juan waited for the ball. It seemed to hang in the air forever. He prepared himself for the catch. The ball spun closer. It was headed straight for his chest. He opened his arms to catch it.

The ball hit Juan's body hard. He tried to hug it with his arms, but the ball had come in too fast. It bounced off his pads and flew straight up into the air.

A Giants player was steps away. The defender grabbed the ball and fell to the ground. It was an interception.

Juan and the rest of the Raiders' offense ran off the field. "Reggie," said Anthony, "what were you thinking when you threw to the rookie? He can't catch."

"He was open," said Reggie. "You had two guys on you."

"That doesn't matter," said Anthony. "Even if there were five guys on me, I could catch the ball better than Juan can when he's wide open."

The players sat down on the bench. Juan looked down at the ground.

Coach Bryant walked over to him. "Catch with your hands," the coach said. "Not with your chest." Juan looked up and nodded. "Don't worry about it," Coach Bryant added.

"Okay, Coach," said Juan.

Juan tried to forget about the dropped pass, but his day didn't get much better. He missed three more passes thrown right at him. On one play, he ran the wrong way and crashed into Anthony. That caused another interception.

Somehow, the Raiders won the game anyway. The final score was 28–7.

After the game, Juan headed to the locker room. Anthony ran up to him.

"Nice job," Anthony said meanly. "Next time, all those dropped passes could cost us the game."

Reggie sprinted up to them. "Leave him alone," he said. "He tried his best."

"If that's his best, I'd hate to see his worst," said Anthony. He shook his head and walked away.

Juan walked slowly to the locker room. He was surrounded by Raiders, but he felt like he was all alone.

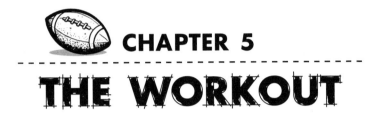

CHAPTER 5

THE WORKOUT

The next day, Juan and Lydia sat on the 50-yard line of the football field. Lydia was helping Juan learn his plays.

Lydia looked up from the playbook. "Oh no," she said.

"What?" asked Juan. "Did I get the play wrong?"

"No, look," she said. Lydia pointed over Juan's shoulder.

Anthony and Reggie were walking onto the field. Reggie had a bag of footballs over his shoulder.

"Should we go?" asked Lydia.

"No," said Juan. He stood up. "I need to deal with these guys."

"You two ready to clear off the field and let us take over?" asked Anthony.

"I don't think so," said Juan.

"Is that right?" asked Anthony.

"Yeah," said Juan. "Maybe we could practice together."

Anthony laughed. "Oh, you're not ready for that," he said.

"Well, if you're so good and I'm so bad," said Juan, "you should be able to teach me a thing or two."

"I don't have time, Rookie," said Anthony. "You should train somewhere else."

"You're not a team player, Anthony," Lydia said. She stood up as tall as she could.

"What are you talking about?" asked Anthony.

"She means that a team player would want to help his teammates get better," said Juan.

Reggie nodded. "The kid has a point," he said.

"You want to beat the Falcons on Saturday, don't you, Anthony?" asked Lydia.

"Of course," said Anthony. "They've won the championship three years in a row."

"You said it yourself, Anthony," said Juan. "My bad playing could cost our team the win next time."

Reggie dumped out the bag of balls he'd been carrying. "Rookie's right," he said. Let's help him out."

"Okay, Rookie," said Anthony. "But if you can't keep up, I'm done. Got it?"

"Got it," said Juan.

"Okay," said Anthony. "Watch this. Reggie, let's do the Workout."

Reggie grabbed a football. Anthony lined up next to him and waited.

"Hut!" yelled Reggie.

Anthony sprinted five steps. He turned to look for the ball just as Reggie threw it. Anthony caught the football. Then he dropped it at his feet.

Reggie reached for another ball. Anthony ran across the field. Reggie gunned another ball at him. Anthony caught it. He let that one fall, too.

Reggie grabbed another ball. Anthony ran back and forth across the field while Reggie fired pass after pass to him. Anthony caught every one.

"Deep!" yelled Reggie. Anthony took off down the field. Reggie waited. Then he threw the ball as hard as he could. Anthony raced down the field, running full speed. Then he reached out his arms and caught the ball.

"Wow," said Juan.

"We call that the Workout," said Reggie. "Think you're ready for it?"

"Oh, he's ready for it," said Lydia.

Juan laughed. He wished he were as confident as Lydia was. "We won't know until I try, right?" said Juan.

"No, we won't," said Reggie, smiling. "Your turn."

"Hut!" Reggie yelled.

Juan ran straight down the field. After five steps, he turned and looked for the ball, just like Anthony had. Reggie threw a hard pass right at him. Juan stuck out his hands, but the ball bounced off.

"It's all right!" shouted Lydia from the sidelines.

Juan looked at Anthony. "Keep going!" Anthony yelled.

Juan left the ball on the ground and raced to his right. Reggie gunned him the ball as he ran.

Juan missed that catch, too. Frustrated, he turned and ran the other direction. Reggie threw him another ball. Again, Juan missed it.

"Come on, Juan," shouted Lydia. "You can do it."

Juan gritted his teeth. He was getting really frustrated. Would he ever be able to catch the football?

CHAPTER 6

GETTING SKILLS

Juan ran back and forth, back and forth. Reggie kept passing him the ball. Juan only caught two passes.

"Deep!" yelled Reggie. Juan took off as fast as he could down the field.

Reggie waited. Finally, he flung the ball high into the air. Juan turned to look. The ball was coming down fast. If he was going to catch it, he was going to have to stop running.

He tried to stop, but he slipped on the grass and fell. The ball bounced on the ground a few yards behind him.

"Whoops, sorry!" yelled Reggie.

Juan scooped up the ball and ran back toward the group.

Reggie laughed. "He's too fast," he said. He turned to Juan. "You outran the pass. I can't throw that far."

"Okay, Rookie," said Anthony. "You need a lot of work. Your speed is solid, but your hands are like rocks. Come on, I'll show you."

"Okay," Juan said.

"You have to get your hands ready to catch the ball," said Anthony. "You can't just hold them up and hope."

Anthony put his hands up in front of his face. "Get your thumbs together and point your other fingers toward the sky," he said. He showed Juan what he meant.

Juan followed what Anthony did. "Like this?" Juan asked.

"Yeah, that's good," said Anthony. "Now turn your hands so that they are facing each other. Then bend your wrists back."

Juan did as he was told.

"Throw him one, Reggie," Anthony said.

Reggie threw a ball to Juan. Juan kept his hands in position. He waited for the pass, and then closed his hands around the ball. He caught it.

I can do this, thought Juan.

"You got it," said Anthony. "Good job."

Reggie threw another pass, then another. Juan caught those, too.

"Way to go, Juan!" shouted Lydia from the sidelines.

"Okay, next thing," said Anthony. "You should reach out with your arms a little bit more. You have to be able to see the ball hit your hands."

"Like this?" asked Juan, pushing his hands away from his body.

"Right," said Anthony. "Now let's see you catch some while you're running."

Juan ran back and forth across the field. He didn't catch every pass, but for the first time, he caught more than he dropped.

"That was good, Rookie," said Reggie when they were done. He gave Juan a high five.

Lydia ran onto the field. "Juan, that was awesome," she said.

"We still need to use your speed, Rookie," said Anthony. "That's how you're going to help us beat the Falcons."

"Tell me what I need to know," said Juan.

For the rest of the week, Juan, Anthony, and Reggie practiced every night after dinner. Juan knew that learning how to be a great wide receiver wouldn't happen in a week, but he hoped he could become good enough to help the Raiders beat the Falcons.

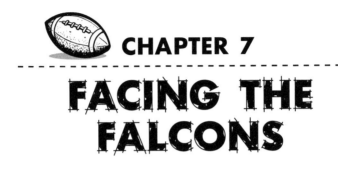

CHAPTER 7

FACING THE FALCONS

Saturday finally came. It was time to face the Falcons. Juan took a seat on the bench. The game was about to begin. He looked back at the bleachers. They were packed. Everyone wanted to see if the Raiders could beat the Falcons.

"Hey, Rookie," someone said. Juan turned around. It was Anthony. "You'll get in the game soon," said Anthony. "Be ready. Think about what we worked on."

"I will," said Juan.

Anthony nodded. Then he raced onto the field with the other Raiders players.

After the kickoff, it was the Raiders' ball. On their first drive, the Raiders struggled to move down the field against the Falcons' powerful defense. After just three plays, the Raiders were forced to punt the ball over to the Falcons.

Juan stayed on the bench as the Raiders lined up on defense. He looked at Anthony. Anthony was playing defensive back. He was covering one of the Falcons' wide receivers.

After the snap of the ball, the receiver that Anthony was covering slipped past him and sprinted down the field. Anthony ran to catch up.

The quarterback threw the ball perfectly. The Falcons' receiver ran under it for a long catch. Then he sprinted into the end zone for a touchdown. After only one play on offense, the Falcons were ahead, 7–0.

"Lucky catch," said Anthony as he came back to the bench. "Just wait until I get back out there."

After the Falcons kicked the ball, Coach Bryant yelled, "Juan, Anthony, Reggie, you're in."

"Our turn, guys," said Anthony.

They sprinted onto the field and joined the huddle. Reggie told the team the play that Coach Bryant had called.

Juan closed his eyes. He pictured the play in his head. He would be running a short route, while Anthony ran a long one.

"On two," said Reggie.

"Wait!" said Anthony. He looked at Juan. "Rookie, let's switch positions," Anthony went on. "I'll run the short route, you run the long one. The Falcons know I'm the top receiver. But they don't know about you. They don't know how fast you are. I'll be a decoy. They'll all think the ball is coming to me, but you'll fool everyone. You run deep, and we'll get a quick touchdown, just like they did."

Juan took a deep breath. "Okay," he said nervously.

"It's fine, Rookie. You'll catch it," said Reggie. "Okay, guys, ready!"

"Break!" everyone said.

Juan jogged to the line of scrimmage. His heart was racing.

He looked down the line at Reggie. Then he waited.

"Hut one! Hut two!" Reggie called. He took the snap.

Then Juan ran. He sprinted past the 50-yard line, then the 40, then the 30.

Juan looked over his shoulder. The ball was dropping toward him. He made one extra burst of speed and reached for the ball. It fell into his hands and stayed there.

He caught it!

Juan cradled the ball with his right arm and kept running. He crossed the 20-yard line. Then the 10. Then the goal line.

Touchdown!

CHAPTER 8

THE FINAL PLAY

Juan ran off the field. Lydia was waiting for him. She gave him a big hug. "Awesome catch, Juan!" she said happily.

Coach Bryant walked over. "Great play, Juan," he said. "But don't relax too long. We're going to need that same effort the entire game if we want to beat the Falcons."

Juan smiled and sat down on the bench. He watched as the Falcons took over.

The Falcons marched quickly down the field. They scored another touchdown just as the first quarter ended. Coach Bryant had been right. Juan's one play was not going to be enough. The Raiders were quickly behind again, 14–7.

Juan started in the second quarter. He still felt great, and he kept feeling better as he caught three more of Reggie's passes.

The Raiders moved the ball to the Falcons' 10-yard line. Because Anthony and Juan had become such dangerous weapons, the Falcons were putting a lot of players on them. That made it easy for Reggie to fake a throw to Anthony on the next play. Then Reggie was able to run the ball himself for the touchdown.

At halftime, the game was tied 14–14.

The Raiders had the ball to start the second half. In the huddle, Reggie called the play.

Juan knew the play well. Anthony and Juan would both sprint straight down the field.

"Let's hit those Falcons quick, boys," said Reggie. "It's time to take the lead. Ready?"

"Break!" said the team.

Juan and Anthony stood five yards apart. "Hut one! Hut two! Hut three!" yelled Reggie.

Juan and Anthony burst forward, but Juan didn't get very far. Two Falcons players jammed him.

Now I'll never get open, thought Juan. *Not with two guys on me.*

Then he realized something. Two guys on him meant no one was covering Anthony. That could be a good thing.

And it was. Reggie gunned the ball to Anthony. He caught it. Then he sprinted forty more yards for the touchdown.

The Raiders were finally ahead. The score was 21–14. And it stayed that way until the fourth quarter. Then the Falcons tied the game, with less than one minute left on the clock.

After three short plays, the Raiders had the ball on the 50-yard line. The score was 21–21. The clock was stopped. There were only six seconds left in the game.

"Okay, time to win this thing," Reggie said in the huddle. He told them the play. Then he said, "We're going long for the touchdown."

"Wait a second," Anthony said. "The Falcons expect that play. They know we're going to go for a long pass to the end zone. Let's give the Falcons something they're not expecting."

"I can't change the play," said Reggie. "Coach calls the plays. That's the play he called."

"Just listen," said Anthony. "If we run something short, the Falcons won't expect it, right?"

"Right," said Reggie.

"Let's throw a short pass to Juan," said Anthony. "I'll block for him, and he'll run for the end zone. With his speed, no one will be able to catch him."

"I don't know," said Reggie. "What do you think, Rookie?"

Juan froze. They wanted him to have the ball for the final play. They wanted him to win the game for the Raiders. Juan closed his eyes.

You're ready, he told himself. *You can do it. Anthony and Reggie believe in you.*

Juan opened his eyes. "Let's do it," he said.

"That's all I needed to hear," said Reggie. A huge grin formed on his face. "Okay, ready, everybody?"

"Break!" the team yelled.

Juan ran to the right side of the field. Sweat poured down his face.

He tried to ignore the sounds of the screaming fans. He tried hard to just think about the play.

It was the last play of the game. It might be the most important play of his life. The game was riding on him.

"Hut one!" yelled Reggie.

Juan took five steps straight ahead. Then he stopped quickly.

The defender got faked out and kept running down the field. Anthony had been right.

When Juan turned, the ball was almost to him. He reached out his hands, thumbs together, and caught the ball.

Juan turned up the field. A Falcons defender was rushing at him. In an instant, Anthony dove in front of the defender and knocked him to the ground.

With Anthony's great block, the field was wide open. Juan took off.

Juan thought about the 200-meter sprint. He knew how to run.

Relax, breathe, take long strides, he thought. He looked at the end zone. He could make it.

Just then, a Falcons defender started closing in on him from the left side. Juan ignored him and tried to think about track. He just kept pushing toward the end zone.

The Falcons player was getting closer. Juan's running skills took over.

He told himself, *Relax your shoulders, lean forward, breathe.* He put all his thoughts and strength into reaching the end zone. *I can do it,* he thought. *I can do it. Relax, breathe, take long strides.*

Juan crossed the 20-yard line, then the 10. The Falcons player dove for Juan's feet, but Juan pulled ahead.

He crossed the end zone just as time ran out.

The Raiders had won! They had beaten the Falcons, 28–21.

As the Raiders celebrated, Lydia ran onto the field. She gave Juan a hug. "You did it, big brother," she said. "You won the game!"

Reggie and Anthony ran up to the two of them.

"Like I said, Rookie," said Reggie. "You've got wheels."

"You got that right," said Anthony.

Juan gave Anthony a high five. "Not a bad block for a wide receiver," Juan told him, smiling.

Anthony laughed and gave Juan a hug. Then he said, "Not a bad catch for a track star."

ABOUT THE AUTHOR

Chris Kreie lives in Minnesota with his wife and two children. He works as a school librarian, and in his free time, he writes books like this. Some of his other books include *The Curse of Raven Lake, Tennis Trouble,* and *Wild Hike.*

ABOUT THE ILLUSTRATOR

When Sean Tiffany was growing up, he lived on a small island off the coast of Maine. Every day, from sixth grade until he graduated from high school, he had to take a boat to get to school. When Sean isn't working on his art, he works on a multimedia project called "OilCan Drive," which combines music and art. He has a pet cactus named Jim.

GLOSSARY

assistant (uh-SISS-tuhnt)—a person who helps someone else do a task

competition (kom-puh-TISH-uhn)—a contest

confident (KON-fuh-duhnt)—having a strong belief in your own abilities

decoy (DEE-koi)—someone who draws attention away from someone else

frustrated (FRUHSS-trate-id)—feeling helpless or discourged

improve (im-PROOV)—get better

position (puh-ZISH-uhn)—the place where something is

rookie (RUK-ee)—someone who is new to a group

signal (SIG-nuhl)—send a message

sprint (SPRINT)—to run fast

strides (STRIDEZ)—steps

surrounded (suh-ROUND-id)—covered on all sides

TWO-SPORT ATHLETES

Not many professional athletes can claim fame in two sports. However, Bo Jackson and Deion Sanders both played football and baseball. They are well remembered for their multi-sport talents.

Bo Jackson was a running back for the L.A. Raiders. He was an outfielder and designated hitter for three baseball teams throughout his career.

Deion Sanders was a cornerback for five football teams. He won two Super Bowls. Sanders started his baseball career with the New York Yankees and went on to play outfield for three other baseball teams.

FOOTBALL WORDS
YOU SHOULD KNOW

defense (DEE-fenss)—the team that doesn't have the ball

down (DOUN)—a single play; a team gets four chances (or downs) to move the ball 10 yards

end zone (END ZOHN)—the last 10 yards at either end of the field

field goal (FEELD GOHL)—when the ball is kicked through the goalposts

huddle (HUHD-uhl)—gather in a group

interception (in-tur-SEP-shuhn)—when a defensive player catches a ball meant for an offensive player

line of scrimmage (LINE UV SKRIM-ij)—the place where the teams line up before each play

offense (OFF-enss)—the team that has the ball

tackle (TAK-uhl)—to knock or pull a person to the ground

touchdown (TUCH-doun)—when the ball is carried into the other team's end zone

sidelines (SIDE-linez)—the lines that run down the long sides of the field

DISCUSSION QUESTIONS

1. Why is Anthony mean to Juan in the beginning of this book? Does Juan handle it the right way?

2. Anthony and Reggie practice with Juan. What are some other ways to make a new kid feel at home at your school?

3. Many athletes play more than one sport. What are some ways to learn new skills when you're trying out a new sport?

WRITING PROMPTS

1. Juan was a track star, but at his new school, he's on the football team. Write about a time when you tried something new, even though you weren't good at it right away. What happened? How did it make you feel?

2. Juan and his little sister, Lydia, get along well. Write about your sister or brother. If you are an only child, write about what you think it would be like to have a brother or sister.

3. Sometimes it's interesting to think about a story from a different person's point of view. Try writing chapter 3 from Anthony's point of view. What does he think about? What does he see and hear?

INTERNET SITES

Do you want to know more about subjects related to this book? Or are you interested in learning about other topics? Then check out FactHound, a fun, easy way to find Internet sites.

Our investigative staff has already sniffed out great sites for you!

Here's how to use FactHound:

1. Visit *www.facthound.com*

2. Select your grade level.

3. To learn more about subjects related to this book, type in the book's ISBN number: **9781434212016**.

4. Click the **Fetch It** button.

FactHound will fetch the best Internet sites for you!